Extant

By Jen Selinsky

Published by Silver Rose Press, LLC in the U.S.A.
812-371-4128
silverrosepress.com

ISBN: 978-1-958792-35-3
Edited by Marla Williams VanHoy
Cover by Donna Cook

Table of Contents

Chapter 1 4
Chapter 2 8
Chapter 3 12
Chapter 4 16
Chapter 5 22
Chapter 6 28
Chapter 7 30
Chapter 8 34
Chapter 9 36
Chapter 10 38
Chapter 11 40
Chapter 12 42
Chapter 13 46
Chapter 14 48
Chapter 15 50
Chapter 16 56
Chapter 17 58
Chapter 18 62
Chapter 19 68
About the Author 72

Author's Note

I had written and then submitted Extant to my previous publisher before the COVID-19 pandemic began. When it was time for my work to be published, during the spring of 2020, I told the publisher to hold off releasing the book for nearly a year because I didn't want to upset anyone further regarding the recent and tragic events of the pandemic. This book is dedicated to all those who have lost their lives, or have been in any other way affected, by COVID-19.

Even though I don't know
How much time
I have left on this Earth,
I take comfort in
The fact the human race
Is a strong and
Durable race.
And though some of us
Will fall during a crisis,
The ones who will remain
Will be there to help
Each other up.

Chapter 1

Some say the human race is already dead. It appeared evident by the way we'd portrayed ourselves, mindlessly performing tasks as we went about the rigors of our daily lives. Some seem to get no joy out of their routines; they feel they must fully commit themselves to the structure.

Then, there were the others who know there is a way out, a way that would allow them to live their lives to the fullest. Those were the ones who truly committed themselves to happiness and all the good things which people seek.

Their minds are not bogged down with the modern ways of thinking and technology, so that means they are free to do whatever, whenever they wanted. Those who truly knew what it was like to be alive.

I let my hand land with a thud down on the desk. The essay my contemporary issues teacher had assigned us was due tomorrow, and I had barely even gotten started. Why would Mr. Wagner assign us a piece in which we had to discuss the modern lifestyle when all of us had not lived more than seventeen, or eighteen, years?

Having to write an essay about conformity is a slap in the face, especially when each and every one of us know we have to live it every day. At that moment, I was not truly alive, and I didn't think there was anything I could have done about it.

Ironic, isn't it? I thought as I sighed.

I wanted nothing more than to stop working on the stupid project so I could relax and watch a little TV. There was no way that could have happened at the moment, however, because I needed to finish the ridiculous essay.

With another sigh, I resigned myself to my fate, and I resumed pumping the laptop keys with my fingers. Finishing the paper was not going to be a fun, or an easy, task.

Nearly two hours later, I had finally completed the assignment. I won't lie and say it was a bad feeling. In fact, it was quite the opposite. Much like the psychologists who had practiced operant conditioning, I bestowed a reward upon my subject. In this case, the subject was me; TV and a bowl of potato chips, well-earned!

I was glad my parents were young and cool enough to have streaming apps, such as Netflix. This time, I let out a sigh of relaxation when I brought up my favorite show, Stranger Things, and began to watch. I thought about my parents as I saw Winona Rider's image on the screen. I guessed people in their late forties weren't so bad, after all.

Sandi and Dave, my older brother and sister, would have agreed with me, but they were both away at college. I'd be next, and my parents would be empty nesters. I didn't think they'd mind that too much, being they were only married for a little over a year before Sandi came around. Then, Dave made his way out of Mom's womb nearly two years later. I was the third, and the last, child to emerge, a year after that. Even though my parents never actually came out and said it, they decided three children were enough, so their procreating days were over.

I couldn't wait to get out of school, even though that would mean even more school after only about three months. I'd been accepted into the Columbia University earlier this year, so that made my parents happy. (More conformity to make me feel less alive.) But ultimately, the good education I would receive there would lead me to a place where I could work to pay my bills in the future.

After I finished watching a few episodes of Stranger Things, I contemplated what I wanted to do for the rest of the day, but nothing else really came to mind. Now I was free to do whatever I pleased, it didn't seem as fun anymore. Also, I felt strangely lost without some kind of routine to follow.

All those points, and more, I had brought up in my essay. Should I have added something extra? Then, about a dozen other thoughts began running around in my head, but they were interrupted by Mom coming into the room.

"Hey, Jules. Did you finish that essay?"

"Yes, finally," I sighed. "I wish I had started on it earlier, but it's a little too late for that. Now, I finally have a chance to test all the theories which I had written down."

"Good, but you probably should have gotten started earlier. Like they always say, 'Never put off until tomorrow what you can finish today.'"

"I know," I replied. How many times did I have to hear that stupid phrase? At least a hundred times during my lifetime, as far as I had counted.

"Well, Dad will be here soon. Did you have any dinner plans for tonight?"

"Not really," I replied, not even having to think about it. Mom and Dad knew I sometimes liked to go out with my friends just to, you know, break the monotony. Tonight, however, was one of those nights when I would have to be void of their company and face the boredom of a family dinner.

Dinner was silent, just as it usually is most nights. We had chicken casserole, but Subway would have been just fine. I'm not very picky when I'm hungry, just as long as I get something into my gut.

Most nights, I can even go for a second helping; after all, I'm still a growing kid. But something was different tonight. The hunger easily subsided and made me feel something else instead, but I wasn't quite sure what. One could call it unsettling, and I would even go so far as to say that, but I couldn't quite pinpoint what exactly it was. Hopefully, it was just nerves, or some sort of passing feeling.

I spent a little more time just sitting in my room after dinner, doing nothing much in particular. It seemed to match the pace of the day as it blended into the night.

When it was time for me to go to sleep, my head hit the pillow, and my weary bones were given a chance to rest.

Chapter 2

I awoke the next morning without hardly any recollection of what had happened late last night. I didn't recall dreaming, or even taking the average seven minutes to fall asleep. Most people might not have found that kind of thing odd, but I was accustomed to lying awake for at least a few moments before I finally drifted off. There was nothing like that last night; I had just lost consciousness almost right away.

***

It was time to get myself ready for school. Shower, check. Now, it was time to put on my clothes and brush my hair.

I looked at my reflection in the mirror after every strand of hair was neatly combed. I thought nothing of my morning routine until I looked up again and noticed something strange.

My face was pale white, as also appeared to be the rest of me. My first response was panic, because I knew my eyes weren't playing tricks on me. How could my skin tone have changed overnight? Nothing about that made any sense.

Next, I stripped off all my clothes to see if there were anything else wrong with my body. After I inspected myself in the mirror again, I was greatly relieved when I found nothing else, but the whole pale white thing was really bothering me. I'd done nothing different during the last few days, so there was no Earthly explanation for that.

I knew I had to put it behind me because I had to drive to school, the last thing I wanted to do right now. But maybe, I would find out something more once I arrived there.

After I'd put my clothes back on, I headed out to quickly say goodbye to my parents. They were in the other room, so I was glad they didn't see me.

My hand was on the doorknob, and I was ready to go outside to my car, when my mother's words stopped me.

She placed her hand on my shoulder. "Jules, honey, I think you'd better come into the living room."

Her tone sounded overly urgent, and I knew something major was up. I slowly turned to look into the faces of both my parents, horrified at what I saw.

Both of them had pale skin as well, but theirs was much worse. They almost looked like albinos.

"Mom, Dad!" I exclaimed. "You guys, too? What's going on here?" I fought the urge to hyperventilate, as I knew it would do me no good. Panic never helps during any situation, especially a dire one.

Neither one of them said anything, but walked back to the living room.

My instinct told me to follow them.

The TV was switched on to ABC, and my heart plummeted when I first heard the female news anchor speak.

"Thousands are dead in the United States alone. News from other countries indicated the death toll reaching up the thousands, as well, equaling then surpassing our own numbers. Scientists believe an outbreak of a deadly virus has caused what is almost now ten-thousand deaths worldwide..."

The anchor continued with the report, but I was too horrified to listen to any more.

Mom quickly turned off the TV. She didn't feel any of us needed to listen to whatever else the anchor said. I wanted to know more, but I also knew neither one of my parents could bear it at the moment.

I had so many questions which my mind was barely able to formulate; I needed to find out what was going on. It was the worst thing I'd ever heard about in all my eighteen years; it was something along the lines of the Bubonic Plague. It sounded like almost half the world's population had been wiped out already!

I looked over at Mom and Dad, who both had tears in their eyes. It appeared their condition was far worse than mine, and I would have given anything to make them feel better. I also couldn't help wanting to get into their minds so I could know what they were thinking.

The three of us sat silently and held on to each other. Given we had just received the most tragic news in the modern world, we didn't think there was anything else we could do.

The sad thing is this is the closest I had been to my parents in months. The three of us usually lived our lives independent of each other, which was far too common in today's world. Now, who knew what the world would be like tomorrow, and how many of us would be alive to see it?

I didn't even ask if there were school, or work, today. And, even if there were, who cared? There were many more important things which the remaining population had to focus on.

Chapter 3

Some days had passed, and we found out no one in our subdivision was affected. Mom was particularly glad because she liked those with whom we shared our neighborhood.

I was beginning to feel everyone left in the entire world should be neighbors. The news had only been marginally depressing during the last few days now the first blow had been struck.

The deaths all over the world still continued; head doctors indicated it was some kind of pandemic. No attacks of terrorist biological warfare had been reported, which was a good thing; too bad it had to take nearly ¼ of the world's populations dying for people to abandon their violent ways!

One week after the incident, and the world was still far from going back to normal. School and government had started back up; many of us were trying to sweep things under the carpet.

Mom and Dad spent a lot of their time in the bedroom, and it was really disconcerting because it wasn't like them at all.

I'd often walked by there and thought I heard crying, but I knew better than to knock. If there were something important enough they wanted to tell me, then they would do so in their own time.

School was now nothing more than a daily ritual, not that it was much of anything before. I also had a hard time even talking to my friends; all those careless, fun times we'd had together now seemed like nothing but distant memories. The thoughts I used to have had died, as so many other people had recently.

It really hit home when I really talked to a few of my friends, and some of them actually told me they knew people who died with this freak virus, or whatever it was.

Our family were fortunate in the respect no one whom we knew seemed to be affected by it. One thing which made me sick was the fact Mom and Dad's skin seemed to look even paler.

They seemed fine, even though their skin had moved past the albino phase and was now right in ghostly white. It really bothered me, the fact they never reciprocated my genuine concern, at least regarding their status. Why do parents do these things to their children, especially when hiding the truth hurts them more? I thought. Even if I were no more than five years old, I would have known something was wrong.

Even if Mom and Dad thought they had to take it to their graves in order to protect me, they had to know what they were doing was wrong. There must have been a way they could feel it in their bones.

Two of my best friends, Shelly and Tim, had also noticed my strange withdrawal. Sure, they tried to gain my interest with normal conversation about their home lives and other things like that, but the subject always went back to death.

Chapter 4

It had been two more weeks, and I hadn't heard any more devastating news. Many who had been struck with the strange virus appeared to be getting better, including Mom and Dad.

The three of us tried to recreate our lives to the days since before the whole terrible thing had started. We became much closer, and each new day was a precious gift. Our little family had been growing and maturing in ways which made us more mindful than we ever were before.

But despite our greater efforts to communicate, we'd conveniently avoided conversations about the future and what it held for humanity. It was my thinking which indicated, because no one knew what was going to happen, we'd all keep our mouths shut, but the opposite had happened, as many around us had chosen to speak of the future, nonetheless.

Many officials across the globe were still struggling to find means of permanent operation. The death toll had taken its sharp knife and carved openings which left a great void. Thousands and thousands of "new" jobs have been created, including one at Burger King, where I worked.

I still shudder to think one of the day managers, twenty-two-year-old Carly, was now gone. I felt the sorriest for her because she was on her way out of the fast-food franchise, earning a college degree in chemistry.

Most of us were high school kids, so we didn't have many great plans yet. I couldn't even think about a college major, especially now, because who knew what else would change between now and then?

At school, I was relieved to find none of our teachers assigned us any superfluous, or tasteless, homework. What I mean by that is the teachers decided to finish their regular curriculum.

In a way, that was a good thing because life was finally returning back to normal, whatever that meant. The tastefulness of it is the fact none of the teachers assigned us any projects regarding the recent, terrible circumstances. It was a relief to know we did not have to analyze any recent occurrences like they were from pages in a history book.

Although, in my English lit. class, everyone spent the entire period going around the room and telling how we all felt about everything. I wanted to be more open, like the others, but I couldn't get the right words to come out of my mouth, especially when I thought about Mom and Dad. It was still all too personal.

Both of them claimed they had been feeling better lately, and I did notice a change in their skin tone. But there was still something different about them, something which made them feel lethargic, especially Dad.

It took everything I had within me not to mention it to either one of them, fearing it would only make things worse.

***

We were having another family dinner, only this one was silent. I missed the lively conversations which we had become so accustomed to before all this, even if they were boring.

I'd been holding my tongue for too long; I knew it was finally time to break my silence. "Mom, Dad. I've been really worried about you guys lately. If something were wrong, you'd tell me, right?"

Both of them looked over at me, appearing as though I had caught them off guard.

"Jules, there's really nothing to worry about. Your dad and I are doing just fine. It's just the recent events have taken a toll on us. The entire world is changing, and we're not really sure how to react, or what to do."

I nodded, indicating I was at least trying to understand. All the while, Dad had remained silent. I had to call him out on it.

"Dad, I can't help but notice how quiet you are lately. Is there something you want to tell me?"

My father sighed. "Jules, honey, your mother is right. Sometimes, there are things better left unsaid."

The scowl which had been on and off my face during the most recent days was back. If there was one thing I hated, it was being lied to, especially by my parents. The least they could do was tell their third-born child what was on their minds.

"Come on, guys. It's like you always say; you can tell me anything. I don't want to think we're keeping secrets from each other, especially about anything important."

"Dear, you know your father is right," my mother stated, pretty much saying the same thing Dad had. "There are certain things that should remain unsaid, at least, until there's a right way to say them."

Indicative by the tone of my mother's voice, I knew she meant business. The only way any conversation was going to progress would be if we changed the subject.

We talked for a little while longer, but Mom and Dad tried to keep the conversation light. It wasn't easy, but I knew I had to do the same.

Lately, I had acquired the habit of watching the news. My morbidly curious mind had to know if there had been any more deaths related to this pandemic, and there had been. The most recent death tolls had reached the hundreds, and the newscaster said more people had died due to complications related to Virus X; that's what they were calling it on the news.

One anchor even pondered the thought of the virus intending to wipe out the entire human race, like so many scientists had speculated. That particular thought froze in my mind. I didn't want to think we all could become extinct, but it sounded like that was the virus's main goal.

I still didn't understand how such a thing could have happened, and I prayed for a better outcome.

That night, I was walking from the bathroom back to my room, when I heard more crying and muffled conversation coming from Mom and Dad's room. An inescapable urge to eavesdrop came over me, so I quietly pressed my ear against the door.

"Louise, when can we just tell her?"

"No way, Brett. I don't want our baby to know how sick you are. Given the sad state of the world, Jules doesn't need anything else to make her even more upset."

"But she's our daughter; doesn't she have the right to know?"

"I don't want to tell her anything, yet. Besides, the doctor might still find a way to fix it."

"Louise, it's a malignant brain tumor. There's no way something like that can be fixed."

I had heard enough. I slowly backed away from the door, forming silent tears because I didn't want them to hear me. But part of me wanted burst my way in their bedroom and confront them for keeping such a big and terrible secret from me.

By the time I had gotten back to my room, I went from forming silent tears to angry tears. I didn't even want to talk to either of them right now, and I wasn't sure how long it would take for me to change my mind.

Because we had already finished our dinners, I figured there was no point in me coming out of my room for the rest of the evening. If either of them wanted to really talk, then they knew where to find me.

Chapter 5

School was now nothing but a forced ritual. Most people my age still looked forward to graduating, despite all that was going on. There were only a few months left until I had to go out and face the world, a world which had already been damaged long before I was even born.

I was executing the monotonous task of walking to my next class, when I felt a tap on my shoulder. I nearly jumped out of my skin.

"Calm down," a more casual friend of mine, Mary, said. "It's only me."

"Oh, hey. What's up?"

Mary looked at me quizzically. She could have easily sensed my cool, detached tone of voice.

"Not too much," she replied with more than a hint of sorrow in her voice.

I began to speak again, knowing I was going to say next would be difficult for her to hear. "I thought, maybe, we could get together because we haven't really talked since, well, you know."

"Yeah," she replied. "I don't even know what we're doing here."

I knew what she really meant, and she wasn't talking about school. Her little brother, A.J., died in the midst of the horrible plague. I didn't have any younger brothers or sisters, but it would be just as devastating if I lost my older ones. I couldn't even begin to imagine what her family must be going through.

"It's like these people around here expect us to go on living, like nothing ever happened, and it's just not like that!" she exclaimed.

I felt the same, but I also didn't want to tell Mary that's what she was supposed to do. That's what we are all supposed to do, even though I certainly couldn't compare to anyone who had lost someone important in their lives.

Even though we'd resolved to talk during lunch, Mary and I had pretty much stayed quiet throughout the rest of the period. I surely didn't want to mention A.J., or anything else which might upset either one of us. Besides, the way we were silently talking led us to believe the old saying; sometimes silence really does speak volumes.

***

I trudged through the rest of the day like most people had. And when I did manage to see a happy face, or two, I wanted to punch them. Yes, it might have seemed like I was going against my own words about moving on, but I also thought no one's happy face should make others feel sick.

I still had no clue about my skin pigmentation, and why it changed the way that it did. There were now too many other important things to think about, like how not to feel awkward in my own home.

All that stuff, and more, was crossing my mind when I was walking home from school. I knew I should have driven, or taken the bus home, but the distance was short enough my leg muscles would not burn too much from the exercise.

My brain kept on going at its usual fast pace, when I lost my balance and fell into the mud that was right in my path.

It was possible I had just lost my footing, but it really felt like I was pushed.

More embarrassed than anything else, I was ready to pick myself back up again, when I heard a sharp whistle and heavy footfalls retreating in the opposite direction.

Perhaps the shrill sound scared away whoever knocked me down, but he, or she, was gone before I even got a good look. The mud was very slippery, and I had to prop myself up on my elbows before I even got myself back up on my feet.

I was now a walking mud monster, or something one would see in a classic horror movie.

Either way, I hoped I would be able to sneak into the house undetected. Dad might still be at work. Getting around Mom would be a different story. Our relationship had definitely seemed to change after the whole world so recently began to fall apart, and she was definitely more overprotective of me now.

Luckily, I managed to slip inside the house almost completely unnoticed. I closed the door quietly and carefully took off my sneakers to avoid tracking in mud, or anything.

I tiptoed up to my room and managed to remove my clothes. I didn't quite know what to do with them because they were caked with mud.

After looking around the room for something to put them in, I found a dirty towel which was lying on my floor.

As I observed the rest of my room, I discovered I was not the only one who was a mess. Clothes, magazines, and other things were scattered around all over the place. Under any other kind of circumstance, it would have almost been funny.

After wrapping up some of the mess in the towel, I tiptoed out to the guest bathroom. Mom was still busy in the kitchen, so I knew that would buy me a little time.

She did hear me, however, and told me it was almost time for dinner.

"Okay," I replied right before telling her I was going to take a quick shower. I needed to wash off both the literal and the metaphorical dirt.

Dad would be home soon, so our tiny family unit would be together again.

I hoped neither Mom, nor Dad, would ask me why I wanted to take a shower but, even by the standards of today's helicopter parenting, that would have been seen as just a tiny bit intrusive.

The shower felt good from the instant I stepped inside. My fingers massaged the shampoo into my grateful hair, which would soon be rid of the partially dried mud.

Cleansing, drying off, and redressing did not take nearly as much time as I had thought it would. It didn't even actually occur to me Mom was holding dinner until we both got home.

Dad was back and downstairs watching TV. Mom must have deduced something was happening as soon as I was one minute late coming home from school, so much for being subtle; I should have gotten a prize for being stupid!

Of course, both Mom and Dad expressed their concern and asked me why I was late coming home from school, was anything wrong, etcetera?

I had to explain my strange compulsion to walk home from school, but I couldn't quite tell them about my having fallen in the mud; that much was evident as soon as I saw the concern mapped all over their faces. Even I couldn't explain it; I hardly even wanted to think about it.

Chapter 6

Days had passed, and there was nothing eventful, that is, except for all the horror featured in the news. There had been more deaths, but the worst part of it all was the fact more fighting and violence started to break out again.

It made me almost sick to my stomach, as I was sure it did many other people. I'd noticed my complexion had been changing back and forth over the past few weeks, and I wondered if other's did the same, as well. If so, then they hadn't said anything.

Mom and Dad still hadn't changed back to their normal hues, and I didn't want to be the one to alarm them.

I didn't notice quite as many changes with others outside my circle, but then again, I wasn't really paying attention.

The best advice someone could give me was to move on, which was what many had been trying to tell me. I knew those words shouldn't have made me angry, but they did. I also knew slowing down and mourning the decline of the human race would only set us back, but that's all I felt like doing since I'd heard about all the most recent violent breakouts. My mind has been doing a lot of thinking and philosophizing lately, and none of it good.

John, Amanda, and Kelly are three of my friends whom I've known since childhood. Before all of this got started, we used to hang out together, being carefree, as most people our age tend to be.

Now, it seems like we are nothing but strangers in the hall. Only every once in a while do we stop to say, “Hello,” or “What’s up?” They had been trying to adapt, and they’ve done a better job so far. Most of the time, it just makes me want to sigh. Life shouldn’t have to be this complicated for anyone.

Chapter 7

I woke up in a cold sweat from a horrible nightmare. The Earth was being taken over by these large creatures of solid magnitude. They had long hair and were dressed like Vikings. Their skin was cracked, and it looked like a bunch of gray rocks mixed together, or they could have also been scales. Either way, my description does not seem to do them justice.

They rode horses and came after people, wielding large swords; it was like something like one would see in an online game, or an M.M.O.R.P.G. Their actions were truly gruesome, and what I dreamt of included things like decapitations and eviscerations. I could go more into detail, but it was terrible enough for me to want to repress the whole thing from my mind.

I wanted to vomit, and I almost did, when something happened; I realized my body no longer felt sick. It was a good thing, too, because throwing up would have only led to my paranoia

I was going to die, like far too many others had.

Except for A.J. and Carly, I still didn't really know anyone who was affected by this "disease." Mom and Dad still looked a little pale, but they had not displayed any telltale signs of sickness.

However, the same couldn't be said for me once I looked at my reflection in the mirror; my skin was a ghostly shade of white. But the thing which bothered me the most were my eyes; they were dark orange. If this was a laughing matter, I would have thought I was a vampire, or something, because of my frightening appearance. After all, even I was aware of all the popular trends in literature, and my otherworldly appearance would have been enough to scare the life out of some people.

My brain was busy still trying to process all this, when I heard a small knock on my door. No doubt, it was Mom and/or Dad coming to tell me something important.

Sure enough, when I opened my door, I found their appearance was similar to mine, as their eyes were green, and their skin was as pale as my bed sheets.

Once Mom saw I pretty much looked like both her and Dad, tears formed in her eyes. She collapsed into my arms and started crying.

I tried, in vain, to console her, but there was nothing more I could do, especially because I didn't even know what was going on. We hadn't heard anything in the news about those mysterious changes, and all our friends and neighbors still seemed fine.

Dad decided to stay home from work, and both Mom and Dad wanted me to skip school so we could spend the day together as a family. Just like the popular saying goes, "No one is guaranteed tomorrow."

Mom was absolutely insistent, as if to ask us what was more important, family or societal obligations.

Because Dad and I knew she had a good point, neither one of us tried to argue with her.

I couldn't help but feel a little sad my brother and sister couldn't join me, but they were safe, undertaking all their collegiate responsibilities. When news of the horrible pandemic broke out, Mom contacted them and insisted they come home. But my siblings, being ever studious, said they would remain on campus, so they did.

Mom, Dad, and I spent almost the entire day talking, but I knew there was still no way I could bring up the mud incident or my recent nightmare. Would I ever be able to tell anyone about that?

Chapter 8

The nightmare came back again, only it was much more intense this time. I was being chased by those strange geo creatures, and I could feel the hair on my skin sticking up and the rising thud of my heart palpitations, like they were going to cause my most vital organ to explode out of my chest!

My fear could have easily been detected, which would have enabled my predators to catch me like an animal. I jolted upright in my bed, but I managed to do so without screaming; that would have clearly woken up Mom and Dad.

I looked at the clock, and it read 5:45, which meant I might as well have stayed up because I needed to get ready for school. I quietly shut off the alarm clock, shuffled into the bathroom, and hopped into the shower.

While Mom didn't forbid me from going to school today, I knew she would have preferred I stay home. So I was not going to have to sneak out, per se, but I made myself feel like I was going on a sneaky mission.

I deliberately decided to walk to school again, to see if anything out of the ordinary happened. Hopefully, another set of my clothes would not have to undergo the ordeal of taking a mud bath. I had to take my other batch out to the backyard and hose them out, which really didn't work all that well. Maybe there was a way I could sneak them into the wash later.

Why was I thinking about my clothes? Certainly, there were so many pressing issues which I should be pondering on concerning my dying species, but my mind couldn't help but come back to something as simple, and as minute, as clothing.

But I wasn't sure if it was only really that because I thought about Mom and Dad. Was I merely worried about upsetting them more than anything in this world could? Was their overall concern for my welfare even greater than their concern for the entire world?

I knew I should have probably purged my mind of those thoughts, but I didn't see much of a chance of that happening right now.

So far, I did not see anything threatening on the way to school, but I only started walking a few moments ago. My mind tended to wander a lot these days, but every normal person's mind does that, especially people living in what felt like a post-apocalyptic dystopia.

Even though none of the news channels had described it as that, I knew the truth. I couldn't help from having visions of my classmates being captured by some of the same barbarians from my dream.

Chapter 9

"No!" I shouted with the loudest breath in my body. "Where are you taking them?"

Upon hearing my cries of distress, one of those hideous creatures made its way over to me.

I tried to run, but not before I saw its face, which looked more like that of a warthog than a man.

Once I got hold of myself, I found I was on the ground and breathing heavily Yet again, I had been on my way to school. If this sequence was nothing but some horrible daydream, then why did it feel so real?

"Are you all right?" I heard a stranger ask as he extended his hand to help me up.

"Thank you," I replied. "I'm fine; I just lost myself for a moment."

The man just smiled and then shook his head, as if he understood. "That's understandable. It's not a hard thing to do when you're living in a world like this one."

I simply nodded and took off in the direction of school. Really, that was the only way I could respond to what he had just said. Even though the encounter was brief, it really felt like that man had delved into my mind and rescued me from something I could not fathom.

I was relieved when I finally reached school, even though nothing there seemed to really change, except for one thing.

Graduation seemed to mean nothing to those hollow, dead eyes in the sea of my peers as they listlessly filed up and down the hallways.

The day went as slowly and painfully as expected by any senior nearing graduation. I still anticipated it, even though it all kind of seemed so pointless now, especially given the uncertainty of the world, and the condition of the human race, which was quickly decreasing.

I decided to take the bus home that day, for safety reasons. Even though my body remained unscathed, my mind was a different story. What if the strange encounter I had today was not only in my head? If it wasn't, then I needed to stay alive so I could tell the tale.

Chapter 10

The death toll was low the following week, except for a few local residents, one of whom happened to be one of our own.

High school senior, Jamie Blair, died from the horrible pandemic. It struck a horrible blow with everyone in the community, especially those who were closest to him. And though Jamie was virtually a stranger to me, I couldn't help but vent my rage over the loss of a young man cut down in his prime. Like most of us had planned, he was going to attend college and make something of his life.

All that made me want to actually make a difference, to grow up to find a cure for this virus. That is, if the human race even lasted that long.

Chapter 11

"Why are you doing this to us?" I asked, shaking my fist, wishing I could land a hit on the creature's jaw.

He picked me up by my collar, and I began thrashing. He laughed at my futile attempt at an escape.

"Your species is weak, coddled, stupid, and neglectful. Whatever little chance of survival you had at the beginning is now gone. This Earth will soon be rid of your kind, to make way for a much worthier species."

I didn't even want to listen to what that hideous gargoyle was trying to tell me. He was absolutely wrong about the human race. Despite the fact our world has seen much hatred, and many wars resulting from that, peace had become a top priority since so many of the overall population was worried about death and complete extinction.

Then, I remembered my current situation, and my eyes burned with anger. How I wished there was a way I could render this alien species extinct, starting with the one threatening me!

Chapter 12

"Your words don't scare me!" I yelled as I woke myself up, thrashing in my bed. Had this whole encounter been a dream, as well? And why was I encountering that same species over and over again?

Even though it was Saturday, I decided to climb out of bed and get dressed. I looked at the clock and saw it was 5:15 a.m. Though I was still tired, I was also afraid of falling back asleep, lest my nightmares take me in a new, and even more horrible, direction.

It was then when I decided to glance in the mirror; I gasped at what I saw. Instead of the yellowish tint my skin had turned earlier, it was now a powder grey, but that's not what had disturbed me the most. My eyes were now dark orange!

It was like something one would see in a horror movie, only everything seemed too real. I wasn't completely transformed, or in any kind of pain; I didn't have some insatiable bloodlust I needed to fulfill by preying on the innocent.

It made me wonder if anyone else had this kind of affliction. And if not, then how was I going to avoid my parents? How was I going to avoid anyone if this didn't go away?

It was inevitable. Mom and Dad came to my door, knocking loudly, and asking me if everything was all right.

I tried to delay them by saying I wasn't feeling very well and I would try to join them for dinner. I really hoped this wasn't going to be some kind of Teen Wolf scenario, where they would come busting in the door, telling me they were suffering from the same affliction. Besides, I knew they already were.

"Okay," Mom acquiesced. "Maybe you should get some rest before you come down to dinner."

Rest? Maybe they didn't know what I had already started to go through, which could be either a good, or a bad, thing. I guessed I would have to bite the bullet and find out when I went downstairs to dinner.

Mom gasped when she first saw the gray color of my skin and my dark orange eyes.

Dad just looked at me with horror and pity, like I was some kind of diseased creature. I should have been the one to give out pity, even though neither Mom, nor Dad, told me about the tumor they had discussed when I overheard them.

"Oh, honey!" Mom exclaimed when she had gathered me into her arms.

I could have said something along the same lines. Both their eyes were still green, and their skin was still the same jaundiced yellow. What did all this mean? Could our bodies have been reacting differently from the virus, that is, if we even have it? Footage on the news of the deceased bodies showed many different shades of colors, so I could not base my assumption on that alone.

Rather than worry about this and talk all gloom and doom, Mom, Dad, and I decided to make the most of our evening. Dave and Sandi also both called to check on us. I breathed a sigh of relief, knowing everyone in my immediate family was still safe. At least, I had hoped.

I tried to keep all our spirits up by talking about graduation, making it seem like the most important thing in the world. Given, it would have been in the light of normal circumstances.

Mom and Dad both listened and did their best to keep me feeling encouraged, but it was evident there was still a lot of fear in the room. Who would have thought, one year ago, any one of us would consider the fact we might not have a future?

Part of me couldn't help but wonder what their minds were thinking, but maybe I didn't really want to know. Perhaps the same was also true for both of them.

Still, we couldn't believe the ceremony was only six days away. This Friday night, I was to become a woman on the verge of venturing out into the world on her own. At least, that was my plan when I got accepted at Columbia.

Now, I wasn't so sure what I wanted to do because recent developments had brought my plans to a screeching halt.

Chapter 13

Things took a more positive turn once we reached commencement. Irene, our class valedictorian, gave a wonderful speech about perseverance and breaking ourselves free from the shackles of fear.

And while Irene did not mention the world's tragic events which changed most of our lives ever so recently, she did a good job reaching us by saying love and understanding were the key components we needed in order to survive.

Irene's speech made me feel guilty about the fact I was ready to give up on myself, so I decided the nightmares, the skin tones, and the strange-colored eyes were not going to get in the way of my dreams! In three short months, I would be ready to take on Columbia University.

My first real day of summer had come and gone with some excitement, but not as much as I'd anticipated. School was out, and I actually found myself becoming a little bored. What was I going to do for the next three months?

Well, I suppose there are worse things than boredom, I thought, knowing the world's been having too much excitement lately. At least the casualties were down again.

Jamie's parents didn't want to have the funeral so close to graduation, thinking it would make everyone too sad, so they decided to have a memorial service next month.

I suppose I should go and give my condolences, even though I hardly knew Jamie, I thought. I knew Mary would be there, as well. I didn't know how she managed to remain so strong after A.J.'s death; I certainly wouldn't be like that if one of my siblings, or parents, passed away. Because I didn't want my mind to think such things, I quickly tried to get myself to conjure up some better thoughts.

Chapter 14

My condition had not changed much during the course of time, but the good thing was I wasn't ailing, at least, according to our doctor. The same was true for Mom and Dad.

The poor man was already baffled enough with all his patients coming in and asking him the same kinds of questions. Evidently, there were tons of people with yellowish skin and strange-colored eyes.

While the doctor himself was not affected, one of his family members was. It must be difficult for him to have to worry about and care for all these other people, I thought. However, he told us we were on his inquiry list if anyone happened to find out any important information.

Chapter 15

I'd planned on today being a normal day, but normal was far from what it really was. Had I known I would have had another terrifying encounter, I would have surely stayed home.

Those horrible creatures were outside again. It seemed like they were patrolling the area, or waiting for someone, and that someone just had to be me!

As soon as they'd spotted me, one of them sauntered over in my direction, wearing a smug expression on his face, or snout, whatever one wanted to call it.

"Do you like what happened to your friend Jamie?" it asked with its pungent bad breath. "That was our work, but I don't mind taking credit for the entire group. If you thought that was good, then you should stick around for the rest of the show. There's plenty where that came from."

"You sick, twisted—" I cut myself off, hurling my body at the creature. As soon as I'd landed on him, I tried to pound him with my fists, flinging obscenities from my mouth.

It appeared there were others who'd gathered outside, but I didn't have time to focus on what they were doing. My overwhelmed mind couldn't help but question why they didn't stop to help, but a part of me couldn't blame them, given the size, and the sheer magnitude, of those creatures. Many of them were probably afraid, and I couldn't really blame them for that. I decided I would be the brave one for all of us.

"Your puny race has no chance for survival," the creature said to me as soon as I'd tried to, unsuccessfully, land a hit on its face. Why did they have to taunt me like this every time they saw me?

It must have been a credo for their strange race, and those words seemed to hurt me more than any physical damage they could have inflicted. I felt myself gasping for air as the words of Dylan Thomas filled my head. There was no way I was going to go gentle into that good night. If this thing was going to eliminate me, then I was going to go out kicking and screaming!

Once I was face down on the ground, I thought I was done, but the sound of a high-pitched whistle had stopped the terrible creature from landing its fatal blow.

"You've won this round, human," it said, sneering. Then, it walked off in the other direction.

Bless that whistling noise; never before was I so glad to hear a sound which reminded me of gym class.

People began staring at me again when I picked myself up off the ground.

Mom and Dad were having lunch with some friends today, which was a good thing because it wouldn't do any good for them to see me in such a state. Now, I would have a chance to get cleaned up and then examine myself in the mirror.

***

As soon as I got home, I did just that. Even though it was hot outside, the warm water streaking down my hair, and skin, felt great. In a way, it felt like a victory wash because the creature had let me live to fight and struggle another day.

However, my positive thoughts then started to dip, especially after I thought of his ugly presence, and how it affected me today.

"Why me?" I screamed, knowing those hideous things could not hear me, at least hoping they couldn't. If I knew for sure they were listening, then I would have loved to give them a piece of my mind and tell them that it was their pathetic race was going down, not our strong one!

That thought, alone, was enough to get me out of the shower.

I dried off and then went into my room.

After looking at my naked reflection in the mirror, I checked my body for any bruises, lacerations, or anything to indicate I needed to try to make another appointment with the family doctor. Luckily, there was nothing to be alarmed about, just a few new bruises started to form, which was expected, because of the beating I had taken.

Not five minutes after I put on a fresh set of clothes, Mom and Dad returned home from their luncheon.

Mom called my name and told me to come downstairs. There was urgency in her voice which I could not ignore.

"What is it?" I asked while running down the stairs.

Dad stood by her side, his hand on her shoulder.

"We need to talk," she told me, looking like she was fighting back tears.

Dad told me to go into the living room, and Mom followed close behind.

They told me to take a seat on the chair facing their couch.

"Is this about my summer plans?" I asked, hoping to diffuse the tension. Then, my mind panicked. They couldn't possibly have known about my encounter today, could they?

Mom simply shook her head and, judging from the sad look on her face, I could tell this was not going to be an easy, or a pleasant, conversation.

Though Mom had done most of the talking, I could see the concern mapped out on Dad's face. He, too, looked like he would begin crying at any moment.

I could have sworn my heart skipped some extra beats as soon as I'd heard this, making the obvious connection.

Mom and Dad were concerned I was going to die, and I could not deny their fears.

When they asked me if I remembered anything about Jamie, I told them I had not seen him in school the last few weeks before graduation. That much was not a lie, Jamie was a person who did not cross my path much, nor was he someone I would have actively looked for.

After Mom asked me more questions about Jamie, I had a few of my own. While a part of me did feel a little bad about talking about Jamie in that way, I figured some education on the subject might, perhaps, help them move in the right direction. Now, I knew I couldn't tell Mom and Dad about my nightmares and my horrible encounters.

There was no way I could have held it together if I mentioned either of those things; this whole ordeal was hard enough as it is.

Chapter 16

It wasn't until after they both insisted I go back to the doctor when I finally acquiesced. We all knew scheduling an appointment was going to be difficult, but no one was more shocked than I when we called the office and the receptionist said he'd had a sudden cancellation today.

The whole notion sounded scary to me, just what was implied by the sudden vacancy. Had one of his patients passed away? I shuddered at the thought of that possibility.

I went upstairs to use the bathroom and splash some cold water on my face.

I was about to head back downstairs, when I got extremely light-headed. With as much strength as I could muster, I tried to shift my body in the opposite direction so I could walk out of the room, but the next thing I felt was my body hitting the floor.

Chapter 17

I came to in a dingy location, not a place which I had ever seen before, nor would I have wanted to. Though it took some time for me to regain all my senses, it did not take long for me to guess what had happened. One of those hideous creatures somehow managed to knock me out and take me from my own home.

I shuddered to think how they got access to me, and what they did with my parents. One of the creatures loomed over me and opened its foul mouth to speak.

If I'd had enough strength, I would have attacked it with everything I had, even though the only actual weapon I could have used was my body. People would have labeled me as a sinister person because of some of the things I was thinking, but I didn't care. That foul race needed to be punished for what it had done to humanity!

"Your puny race shall not survive," this one said, the same as so many of his own stinking brethren.

"What have you done to me; where are my parents?"

"Your puny race shall not survive. I have taken your parents, along with many others. And you shall be next."

It leaned in even closer, dripping saliva from its sharp, yellow-stained teeth onto my face.

I held my breath and tried not to let anger consume me while my desperate mind tried to formulate a plan. I did not feel the excruciating pain until I tried to stand up. I fell back on the ground again; I noticed my leg was broken.

It laughed at my attempt, and then my failure, to get myself up off the ground.

I narrowed my eyes. “It’s a good thing for you I’m incapacitated, or else I would kill you with my own bare hands!”

The creature laughed its horrible laugh again. “What do you intend to do about it? No one is coming to your aide. By the time I’ve said this, we’ve slaughtered hundreds more. Keep me talking, and we’ll overthrow the entire nation!”

I was about to open my mouth to speak again, when I was hit with a second wave of pain. A loud scream came out of my mouth instead, replacing the words which I wanted to say. This pain did not seem to go as quickly, especially because my rage-induced endorphins started to wear off. That was going to leave me in a most vulnerable position, but there was no way I was going to allow myself to just curl up and die!

I moved my body to the left and got into “fighting position.” If I couldn’t kill this thing with my body, then I would have to use my words.

“I don’t care what you, or your kind, say; the human race is durable! Many things have threatened to rid the planet of us, but none have been successful. Hatred such as yours can only pose a threat to those who wish to remain afraid. There is no way you can ever win!”

Instead of having to hear its guttural laugh again, it paused for a moment while its face formed a frown. Could my words have made it start to think I was right?

"Do you mean to think I will spare you with that pathetic little speech you just made?"

Even though those were the words coming out of its mouth, I wasn't subjected to the same confidence which had taken away my hopes just moments ago. Perhaps I had gotten through to its thick skull after all.

"I can't control what you do to me, or my parents, but there is still no way you can win! As long as there are those who are determined, they will band up against you, and then how your kind shall all crumble!"

I didn't know where all those sudden words of bravery were coming from, but I ventured a guess my endorphins had returned. And even though I could still not move much of my lower body, the pain seemed like it was reduced.

"Weak, pathetic human. I knew I should have finished the job last time, but now should be more appropriate, right in the middle of your stupid, little declaration. Prepare to join your ancestors."

I sat up as much as I could, leaning in and daring him to try to take me by the neck. Even if my words had not killed him, they seemed to at least strike a blow to his ego, and I hoped my words would echo in his head long after I was dead. If I had to be taken out by this vile thing, then at least it would be by lesser a fearful means.

The strangest thing happened after it wrapped its large hand around my neck; it didn't seem to be exerting any pressure. In fact, it felt like air was coming in, giving me even more life than I had expected being in a place like this.

Despite the fact it did not hurt, it still felt like I was dying because I could actually see a light right before I felt like my body, or my spirit, was soaring to another place. The blinding light was getting much closer, until I opened my eyes and took a large gasp of fresh air.

Chapter 18

"My baby!" I could have sworn I heard the voice of my mother exclaim in my head, but I wasn't sure it was her until I turned my head to see her standing next to Dad.

"Oh, sweetheart, we thought we lost you!" Dad said, crying tears of relief. "I'm so glad your body was able to fight the infection."

Infection? I thought. Am I in the hospital?

Mom went outside and summoned one of the nurses to go get the doctor.

Moments later, the doctor rushed to my bedside to see how I was progressing. He appeared to be just as relieved as my parents when he saw me conscious.

"What's going on here?" I asked like I was coming out of some morphine-induced coma.

"I don't know where to begin," he replied, sounding both delighted and perplexed.

"Your parents called 9-1-1 after they discovered you fainted. The ambulance brought you here, where I injected you with a serum the government has been working on to try to help all the diseased people.

"You're the first person we've administered the drug to at this hospital. We were hoping

your body, as a result, would conquer the hallucinations and allow it to return to its natural state. It might take a little bit of time, but your skin and your eyes should return to their natural color momentarily. I think some of the gray skin is already starting to turn."

Hallucinations? Was I merely dreaming about those horrible creatures; was any part of that real?

"Then, the creatures..." I began to ask, sounding like I had come from another planet. "None of that was real? The encounters I had with these foul beings who wanted to destroy humanity?"

Instead of looking at me like I should be locked up in the mental ward, the good doctor did his best to answer my questions. "Your brain was clearly affected by the virus, which is now known for causing strong hallucinations. By the time the paramedics had delivered you to me, your body was so infected we didn't know if you were going to pull through."

I then glanced over at Mom and Dad, who looked at me like I was the result of some kind of miracle, which, essentially, I was.

The doctor continued, "But they would have appeared to be real in more extreme cases like yours."

I then felt guilty for not having told my parents about the creatures I'd encountered in my head. I also had the feeling they would gently confront me about it later.

"I know you have just woken up, but it there any way I can get a full account of what happened in your mind, these creatures you saw, and what made them appear so real?" the doctor asked.

Now I knew I wasn't going to be sent to some psych ward, I felt I could rely on both the doctor, and my parents, to take what was about to say very seriously.

"Forgive me," the doctor said after noting my hesitation. "I can give you more time to recuperate. Take a day, or two, if you would like, but the medical community can use a solid statement from one of the first patients we were able to treat. Of course, we will require your permission by having you sign a consent form. I'll leave you to talk to your parents for a while as I go to retrieve one from reception."

The doctor left the room, leaving me to wonder what my folks were going to say to me.

Both Mom and Dad leaned in close for a hug, and it made me feel relieved they were not upset with me.

When they released me from their embrace, Mom gently took my hand.

"We thought we'd lost you," she said, not wanting to let go of my hand. "Why didn't you tell me, or your father, about these hallucinations?"

"I just didn't want to alarm you, as it seemed you were suffering from the same thing I was. It all seemed so real. Could either of you tell I was withholding information from you?"

Mom and Dad nodded in unison just as the doctor came back in with the form. Because I had turned eighteen a few months ago, my parents would not have to approve, or initial, the document, but he showed it to them, anyway.

He then proceeded to go over all the legal jargon and asked me if I had any further questions. He followed that by saying he and one of his staff would be in shortly to record my story on a digital camcorder.

Upon the doctor's return and a nurse's arrival, I explained everything I remembered, right from the beginning, elaborating on all the parts which I thought were important.

One of the doctor's staff members made sure to keep the camcorder focused on both me, and him, during the entire time I was telling my tale.

Mom and Dad both said they didn't need to be in the video, but they decided to stay in the room during the whole thing so they could give me moral support.

Though I had told my story in a matter of minutes, it seemed like even more time had passed, and I had a better understanding of what I'd gone through.

As soon as the doctor had finished interviewing me, he turned the camera to face him and talked about the deadly condition, which the government had just given a name, Andromidia. I had to shudder because there had not been a pandemic this widespread since the Black Plague wiped out nearly half of Europe during the Middle Ages.

After the entire thing was over, the doctor then thanked me for giving my consent to be filmed, and he told us we could go home. Before we left, he also said he would like to check my progress, once a month, to see how I was doing. He then informed us he can offer a year's worth of free doctor's visits for me, with no co-pay on my dad's health insurance.

I told him I would think about it.

The doctor then gave me a serious glance and said he hoped I would seriously consider it.

Chapter 19

Once we arrived back home, Mom and Dad had something they wanted to tell me. It was about Jamie. They'd couple they had met for lunch a while ago mentioned Jamie had suffered from nightmares and hallucinations, just like I had. His skin and his eyes were also the same color as mine. Unfortunately, as everyone already knew, he didn't make it to the doctor in time.

When I tried to ask them what kinds of hallucinations had plagued him, they couldn't give me an answer because they didn't know. I could only imagine his were far worse than mine.

It was going to be a difficult thing trying to settle back into our normal lives after all this, but we knew we had no alternative but to move forward. Part of me still felt like those creatures were out there, taunting me, especially because everything had felt so real. But if I were to give up on my dreams now, then it would have felt like I was giving those foul things the victory. That wasn't going to happen; I would not give up on my plans to attend college and make a life for myself!

Mom and Dad did not take long to come back to their normal selves. Their skin and their eyes became the same color I have known ever since I was born. Since then, they had both gone back to the doctor, who gave them a clean bill of health.

It was such a relief he did not mention anything about my dad's brain tumor, which my parents never actually told me about. It might have taken care of itself either during his brief infection, or his recovery.

My colors were starting to go back to normal, as well. At the moment, both my skin and my eyes were yellow, which was an improvement.

The doctor was delighted because of that, too, especially because I'd agreed to let him monitor my progress and share it with his colleagues.

It was getting to the point where I'd almost become a celebrity in that place. People marveled at me every time I came in, as I was now known as the girl who beat the odds.

Though the new cure was still in the earliest phase of development, it was being used, worldwide, to treat people who had suffered from the highly infectious virus.

Though there were many standard news reports every day, TV anchors, and newspaper journalists reminded us the cure was still in the developmental stages and would often include side effects.

I was well aware of that; I was no longer suffering from any day hallucinations, although I had yet to escape those that came in the form of nightmares.

Sometimes, the creatures came back to my dreams. Other times, I found myself in unimaginable scenarios, but they seemed to recede over time, as did my condition.

Due to my new celebrity status, the doctor wanted to put my story on the practice's website, and the news wanted to do a story about my progress, which I had also okayed.

There were a lot of legal forms and things I had to sign in order to give my consent, but if the retelling of my account was going to help others, then I was all for it. They also told me I would be compensated for my time.

Despite all my fears and anxieties, however, things were starting to get back to normal, whatever could be considered normal these days.

The thing that gives me the most satisfaction is the fact I survived, despite the many things that were stacked up against me. After all, I am young, and I am very grateful for the opportunity to be able to start a new life at college, knowing I have the ability to survive, along with the rest of the human race.

About the Author

Jen Selinsky was born in Pittsburgh, PA. In 2003, Jen earned her bachelor's degree in English from Clarion University of Pennsylvania. In 2004, she earned her master's degree in library science from the same school. Jen is a former librarian, who now solely focuses on her writing career. She has published more than 250 books, many of which contain poetry. She worked as a Senior Editor for Pen It! Publications and also had jobs at Write Your Best Book and with Indie Publishing Group. Jen is a freelance article writer for The News and Tribune, The Butler Eagle/The Cranberry Eagle, and SoIN Tourism, a proofreader at ProofreadingPal, and an editor at Hydra Publications, Crossroads Publications, and BK Roysten Publishing, as well as a beta reader and part of the selection committee for Jumpmaster Press. She also proofreads, edits, ghostwrites, and beta reads books for individual clients. One of her children's books, *You Are You!* won the IMADJINN Award for Best Children's Book 2019. Jen lives in Sellersburg, IN.

www.ingramcontent.com/pod-product-compliance
Lightning Source LLC
LaVergne TN
LVHW010942110826
845149LV00013B/2715

9781958792353